Lily and Lorna

Books in the Red Fox Read Alone Series:

Lily and Lorna

Jean Wills

Illustrated by Susan Varley

RED FOX

To my Mother

A Red Fox Book

Published by Random House Children's Books
20 Vauxhall Bridge Road, London SW1V 2SA

A division of Random House UK Ltd

London Melbourne Sydney Auckland
Johannesburg and agencies throughout the world

First published in 1991 by Andersen Press Ltd
Red Fox edition 1992
Reprinted 1992

Printed and bound in Great Britain by
Cox & Wyman Ltd, Reading, Berks

ISBN 0 09 978340 1

Contents

1
Lady Muck

'*Now then, Mr Wall!*'

Lily knew that voice.

So did her brother Charlie. 'There's the Lobster. I'm off!' He ran upstairs.

CLUMP, CLUMP, CLUMP, CLUMP, CLUMP!

'Is that *thunder?*' the Lobster asked.

'Only that boy of mine,' Pa said. 'Feet like bricks.'

'Don't I know it! Up and down my basement steps. Why isn't he at school?'

'A half-holiday. What can I get for you, Mrs Lobb?'

'Ten pairs of kippers. A dozen cod steaks. Four pints of prawns. Some nice fresh plaice. *And I do mean fresh.*'

Mrs Lobb was cook at the big house up Albert Road. Monday and Thursday afternoons she came down to the High Street to give her orders. All the shop-keepers were very polite. But Mrs Lobb, with her big red face, was rude as she liked.

Lily waited until the Lobster had left their shop, then darted out.

'Where are you off to, Lily?' called her sister Bea from the cash desk. Lily pretended she hadn't heard, ran to the corner and started up Albert Road.

The rest of the afternoon was hers. No school. No jobs.

As she passed the dairy it began to rain. Great big drops like pennies on the pavement.

'Oh, lor! No coat, no nothing.'

She reached the big house.

TAP, TAP, TAP, TAP, TAP!

There was a face at an upstairs window, and a hand that beckoned.

'What can *she* want?' Lily wondered.

The girl who lived at the big house was very grand indeed. She rode around in a carriage and never went to school. Charlie called her Lady Muck.

Lily pretended not to notice, but the rain was really sloshing down. Since the Lobster was safely out of the way Lily ran down the basement steps and crouched by the door.

It opened, and Lily fell inside.

'You're all wet!' said Lady Muck.

'A bit of water won't kill me.' Lily scrambled to her feet. Charlie had told her about the big kitchen. Now she saw it for herself.

'I expect you're hungry too.'

Lily was always hungry, but she wasn't going to tell Lady Muck.

'Follow me.'

Lily didn't move.

'*Please!*'

It wasn't a word Lily expected to hear in the big house. Mrs Lobb certainly never used it.

Close to, Lady Muck was just another girl, like Lily. In for a penny, in for a pound, she told herself, and stepped forward.

10

'Don't make a sound. We mustn't get caught.'

Up through the house they went. Past huge rooms, walls covered with pictures, full of chairs, tables, cabinets, *pianos*.

Lady Muck stopped at last, and crept inside an upstairs room. Lily followed. A table was set for two, but one dinner had barely been touched.

'Eat it,' Lady Muck whispered in Lily's ear.

Lily sniffed. Rabbit pie. Oh, the smell was gorgeous! Her dinner had been ages ago. Leek soup and a bit of fat bacon.

She tucked in, and was just polishing off the last mouthful when a voice came out of an inner door.

'So you've come to your senses, Miss.'

Lily dropped her knife on the plate
and shot down under the table.

A pair of black ankles and feet
appeared. 'Now you may eat your pudding.
Then read while I take a little nap.'
The feet and ankles disappeared.

Lily crawled out and watched Lady
Muck wolf down a bowl of pears and
custard.

Well!

Lady Muck clattered her spoon, picked
up a book and flopped it on the table.

Then she led Lily all over the house. Twice they were nearly caught. Once they escaped on to the terrace. Another time they were trapped for ages behind a sofa, and had to crawl across the carpet to reach the hall.

The big grandfather clock struck four.
'You'll have to go!' Lady Muck took Lily back to the kitchen. 'Old Bedsocks will be waking up.'
'Bedsocks?'

'Miss Bedford, who looks after me. She's no fun at all.'

'Neither's the Lobster.' Lily explained who that was.

Lady Muck giggled. 'Come again tomorrow.'

'Can't. It's school.'

'After then. Promise!'

Halfway down Albert Road Lily met the Lobster. *If you only knew where I've been*, Lily thought as the cook puffed past.

'Well,' said Bea that evening as she put Lily's hair in rags. 'Where did you get to this afternoon?'

'Went to see a friend.'

Charlie nodded. 'Lady Muck.'

'I didn't, so there!'

'Yes you did.'

'Stop that arguing,' Bea said. 'At least Ma doesn't have to hear it.' Ma had died when Lily was a baby. Now Lily was seven, Charlie nine, and Bea seventeen. Bea wound the last ringlet. 'Give us a kiss, and off to bed.'

Charlie and Lily slept in the attic, where the roof sloped and the wind whistled. Cold in winter, hot in summer, it was autumn now and the rain blew in.

Drip, drip, drip, drip . . .

The drips fell into two big pails. In winter they froze over.

Lily put her head on the pillow, but couldn't get comfortable with the knobbly rags. Something touched her neck.

'Charlie! There's another drip!'

'No, it was me,' Charlie said. *'What
were you doing at the big house?'*

'How did you know?'

'I was on the wall, scrumping apples.
And there was my sister, lah-di-dah, up
on the terrace!'

She had to tell him.

Next morning it was still raining. Charlie stuffed newspaper into his boots and clumped downstairs. Lily, her teeth chattering, looked out of the window.

There was Billy, steaming. They couldn't afford a horse of their own. When Pa went to Billingsgate market he hired old Billy from the dairy to pull his cart.

Charlie began to help unload. He had to haul the handcart up Albert Road with the Lobster's order before he went to school.

'*Come on, Lily!*' Bea called. 'There's no holiday today, you know.'

Downstairs the kitchen smelt of hot tea. Bea told Lily to spread the slices of bread.

'Thinner,' Bea said. 'We're not made of money.'

Lily scraped at the grocer's cheapest margarine. *However was she going to see Lady Muck today?*

2
Postman Charlie

'Why do I have to have ringlets, Bea?'

Lady Muck's hair had been straight like Lily's, but tied back with a velvet ribbon.

Bea pulled out a rag.

'OW!'

'You're an ungrateful girl, Lily Wall. I slave day and night to keep you, Charlie and Pa respectable.'

'*They* don't have to have rags in their hair.'

'I clean and cook, wash and sew. And work at the desk. Len says I need glasses.'

Len was Bea's young man. He worked at the Albert Road Dairy.

At last the torture was over.

'There you are. Fit for a princess.' Bea held out the well-darned coat. 'Don't forget your slice. And your brolly.'

Lily put her bread and dripping safe in her pocket, fetched the brolly and said goodbye to Pa and Billy.

Bea had bought the brolly off the
rag-and-bone man. Some of the spokes
were broken, but there was a hole in just
the right place for looking out.

As Lily turned into Albert Road
Charlie charged towards her.

'Out the way!'

The empty handcart rattled past.

A man came out of the dairy yard
leading a horse, the cans on the milk-cart
clanking behind. And here was Len, on
his way to fetch Billy. Len knocked on
the brolly.

'Anybody in?'

Lily giggled. She liked Len. It was a pity he couldn't wait for her to grow up, instead of marrying Bea.

'Get along now,' Len told Lily. 'Do you want those ringlets to fall out in the damp?'

'Yes,' said Lily. 'I DO!'

Len went laughing down Albert Road.

Lily felt proud as she passed the big house. Charlie said it was the grandest in London, after Buckingham Palace of course. And she had been inside!

School was a very different place. There was only one room, and wet mornings meant hanging coats round the boiler to dry. The windows steamed up. Tempers too.

Charlie ran in, late as usual. There was no space left for his coat so he hung it on the blackboard. Rivers ran down over Miss Jones' letters.

'Charlie Wall,' she wailed. *'You clown!'*

'Yes, Miss,' Charlie said.

Everyone laughed. Except Miss Jones.

'Remove it at once!'

As Charlie reached up Miss Jones saw his boots. She made him take them off, and fetched some dry socks from her cupboard. The socks were miles too big. Every time she turned her back Charlie waggled a foot in the air.

It was still raining at dinnertime, so
they had to stay inside. Lily gobbled her
slice and thought of Lady Muck.

She thought about her all afternoon
instead of the lesson.

'Lily Wall, fetch the dunce's cap and
stand in the corner!' Miss Jones told her.

The moment school was over Lily
rushed for her coat and brolly. She
hurried along to Albert Road and
waited for ages, but nobody
came.

Wednesday she decided to
walk straight past. Then a
voice behind her, all in a
rush, said, 'Here I am!'

There stood Lady Muck.

'Yesterday was my music
lesson. I forgot. Sorry.'

Lily saw a superior brolly
with familiar ankles
underneath.

'Here comes Bedsocks.'

'Quick. Take this!' Lady Muck gave Lily a letter.

Instead of going home to read it Lily went into the dairy yard. She crossed the cobbles to Billy's stall.

Billy nudged her, but her pockets were empty.

'I'll read you my letter instead. "Dear Gerl." Look at that, Billy. She can't even spell! "Can you come Satterday? After diner wood be best when Old Bedsoaks takes her littel nap. Love, Lorna." ' Lily stroked Billy's nose. ' "P.S. Give your arnser to the fishboy Friday." '
Well!

Thursday night after Lily had counted twenty drips she said, 'Charlie?'

'I'd just dropped off!'

'Tomorrow's Friday.'

'You woke me up to tell me *that?*'

' 'Course not. Will you take a letter when you go to the big house tomorrow?'

Lily explained.

'*Fishboy?* What a cheek! And now a flippin' *postman!*'

'Please, Charlie.'

'What am I supposed to say? "Wotcher, Mrs Lobb, my good woman. Kindly deliver this letter to Lady Muck." '

'Don't be silly. *She'll* be somewhere. And her name's Lorna.'

'She's Lady Muck to me. I'm not doin' it anyway.'

Lily sniffed.

'Don't start,' Charlie said. Lily sniffed again. 'Oh, give it here!'

'Thanks, Charlie.'

When she woke next morning Charlie was reading her letter.

'Postmen don't do that.'

'This one does. "Dear Lorna, I will come 2 o'clock tomorrer over the wall. Love, Lily." *Love, Lily*,' Charlie mocked. 'And what do you mean by *over the wall?*'

'I can't walk in the front door, can I?'

'Or climb the wall.'

'*You* do.'

'That's different.'

They heard Pa's voice.

'He's back from market, and I'm not down!' Charlie picked up his boots and ran.

'The letter, Charlie!'

He snatched it up.

It was another wet day. More coats to dry in the schoolroom. Steamed-up windows, and bad tempers. As Lily ate her slice at dinnertime Charlie gave her another letter.

'Dear Lily, Meat you by the wall. Love, Lorna. P.S. I will bring a pick nick.'

3
Herring in the High Street

'If I've told you once I've told you a hundred times,' Charlie told Lily. 'She was under the kitchen table. I slipped her your letter. By the time the Lobster had checked the order and done her usual grumble, Lady Muck had written another.'

Lily read the letter again as they crossed the dairy yard on Saturday afternoon. The stalls were clean and empty, the horses still out on their rounds.

Charlie led the way to the far corner and wriggled through a gap in the fence. Lily followed.

'There's the wall.'

Lily looked up. However would she climb it? Something flew over the top. A note, tied to a stone.

' "Go to the gate." What gate, Charlie?'

'There's one further along.'

As they reached it Lorna came out. 'Where can we have our picnic?'

'Follow me,' said Charlie importantly.

He took the basket, led the way through the gap, and into Billy's stall.

They ate a whole fish pie with their fingers, followed by cold jam roly poly. And lime jelly, melted, to drink.

'What a blow-out!' Charlie flopped in the clean straw and tapped his middle. 'That old Lobster might be a dragon, but can she cook!'

'You should have tasted her rabbit pie,' Lily said.

Lorna turned up her nose. 'I think eating rabbits is disgusting.'

'No worse than eating fish.' Charlie wanted to know what the Lobster would do when she found her pie had gone missing.

'She won't suspect me. I'm what's called a fussy eater. Probably she'll blame old Bedsocks, who lives for eating and sleeping.'

'I wouldn't mind a teacher like that,' Charlie said.

Lorna wanted to hear all about school, especially Miss Jones.

'You *are* lucky,' she told Lily and Charlie. They couldn't believe it!

Nobody noticed the milk-cart's return.

'What's this then?'

There stood Len with old Billy.

'Wotcher, Len.' Charlie told him about the picnic.

Len raised his cap at Lorna. 'How do, Miss?'

Then Lorna wanted to hear about Billy. Len told her he pulled the milk-cart, and went to Billingsgate twice a week.

After that it was time for Lorna to go.

'Don't tell Bea,' Lily warned Len.

'Who's Bea?' Lorna asked as they reached the gate.

'Our big sister.'

'I wish I had a sister.' Lorna looked at Charlie. 'Or even a brother.' She opened the gate. 'Next time I want to see your shop.'

'She can't,' Lily told Charlie as they lay in bed that night.

'You saw inside *her* house.'

'That was different. Lorna couldn't come to this tiddly place without anyone knowing.'

'She'll get here somehow,' said Charlie. 'Or I'm a pickled herring.'

Nothing happened on Sunday. Monday.
Tuesday.

After school on Wednesday Lily
hurried down Albert Road in the rain.

'Boo!'

Lily nearly dropped her brolly.

'Don't stop. I'm coming too!'

'You can't!'

But Lorna was running ahead, her
long hair like a horse's tail. Lily didn't
catch up until she reached the shop.

'Who's that with you?' Bea asked as they passed the desk.

'This,' said Lily, 'is . . . ' But a clap of thunder drowned her out.

Charlie came running.

'Told you,' he said when he saw Lorna.

There was more thunder. Rainwater sizzled along the gutters. Pa said in all his years in the High Street he'd never seen anything like it.

Lily took Lorna to the little back kitchen, but there was nothing there to offer a fussy eater.

Charlie went and sneaked some
sprats. They cooked them in the frying
pan, scrunching them up, burning hot.
Then rushed to the cold water tap to cool
their mouths.

Pa shouted, 'I want you out here.'

Off went Charlie.

Lily was worried. 'Suppose someone's
come.'

Lorna shook her head. 'It would take
more than a thunderstorm to wake old
Bedsocks.'

'What about your mother and father?'
Lily had wanted to ask this question ever
since the first day, but hadn't quite liked
to.

'Sometimes I see them in the evenings. Never in the afternoons.'

Lily was trying to imagine seeing Pa and Bea so seldom when she heard a funny noise. A slurping and gurgling and . . .

'The floor's under water!' Lorna cried.

As they jumped on the table Charlie came splashing with bare feet.

'You two get up to the attic and see to them pails!'

They took off their shoes and stockings.
Then Lorna followed Lily upstairs.

The pails were so full they couldn't lift
them. While Lily fetched a bowl Lorna
opened the window.

'Come and see!'

The rain had stopped but the High
Street was full of water. Mr Smith, the
grocer, was up to his knees!

Lily and Lorna emptied half a pail
into the bowl. Four times they staggered
to the window and . . . SPLOSH!

'Bring the pails down here,' Pa
shouted.

'Tuck your skirts into your drawers,'
Bea told them. 'And fill the pails with
fish.'

When they were full Pa carried the
pails upstairs. The floodwater lapped the
top of the slab, but nearly all the fish had
been rescued. Only a few herring floated
away.

Billy splashed along the High Street
pulling the milk-cart. Len saw Lorna.

'What's she doing here?'

'Visiting,' said Lily. 'But now she
can't get home!'

'We'll soon fix that.'

Lorna climbed on Pa's back, and Pa
waded out to the milk-cart. Lily waved
until it had turned the corner.

By the time Len returned the floodwater was going down.

'You've been a time,' Bea said.

Len let out a slow sigh.

'I'm afraid your friend's in a spot of
trouble,' he told Lily. 'A lot of carriages
had piled up in Albert Road. Inside one
was her ma and pa.'

Bea frowned.

'Who was that girl?'

4
Salmon on the Steps

When she'd listened Bea said, 'Beats me why she wanted to come here in the first place.'

'She's my friend,' Lily said.

'Mine too,' Charlie added.

'Just nosy, more like. Wanted to see how the other half lives. Well now I hope she's happy.'

Lily wasn't happy.

After the flood the shop was in a terrible mess. It was hard to believe that water could leave a place so filthy. They scrubbed and scrubbed, until the only smell was disinfectant.

Lily was so tired she fell asleep over the kitchen table. Pa had to carry her up to bed.

Next day Charlie's boots fell to pieces.
He didn't go to school, and neither did
Lily. She helped Bea make fish-cakes
from the fish they'd rescued.

In the afternoon the Lobster came.
Lily and Charlie hid behind the slab.

'*Now then, Mr Wall.*'

The Lobster gave her order, but
nothing was said of Lorna.

'Tomorrow you must find out what
happened,' Lily whispered to Charlie.

'How am I supposed to do that?'

Bea had borrowed a pair of boots for
Charlie. They were big enough for a
giant. 'You'll have to pad them out,' she
told him next morning.

When the handcart was loaded Charlie set off, fell over his feet and banged his head on the slab. A bump came up like a duck's egg.

'He's not going anywhere,' Bea told Pa.

She pulled the rags out of Lily's hair.

'Lily will have to pull the handcart.'

Up to the dairy wasn't so bad, but after the cobbles Albert Road grew steeper. It took Lily ages to reach the big house.

Gathering up the parcels of fish she hurried down to the basement. The steps were slippery from the rain. Out flew the parcels from her hands. And out of the parcels flew the fish!

The door opened and there was the Lobster. All her chins wobbled at once.

'*Where's the boy?*'

'He hurt himself.'

The Lobster didn't care about that. There were dabs on the doorstep. Winkles on the window-ledge. Salmon on the steps.

'I've a good mind to send the lot back!'

'Please don't, Mrs Lobb,' Lily begged.

The Lobster fetched a bowl. After Lily had picked up the fish she had to wash it in the kitchen sink.

'Now put it on the table. *Gently!* Wait while I check.'

There was something under the table. Something which moved . . .

Lily edged closer. A letter was pushed into her hand. She hid it in her coat.

The Lobster sniffed.

'You can go now.'

As Lily left she turned back for a last look at Lorna. Then the Lobster marched forward and the door was slammed in her face.

Lily fairly flew down the hill, the handcart rattling behind her.

'Where've you been?' Bea scolded. 'You'll never get to school on time!' She gave Lily her slice, then turned on Charlie. The bump had gone now. 'And off with you an' all.'

'In *these* boots?' Charlie said. 'Want me to break my flippin' neck?'

Lily felt the letter safe inside her coat. And ran.

'You're late, Lily Wall,' Miss Jones complained. 'You were absent yesterday as well.'

'That was because of the flood, Miss.'

'The storm was the day before. And why isn't your brother here?'

'He's sick, Miss.' Not for anything would Lily tell Miss Jones the real reason.

As though to make up for all the rain, the sun shone in the schoolroom window the whole morning. Miss Jones' pupils grew restless. The boy behind Lily pulled her ringlets.

At dinnertime they escaped into the
playground. At last Lily was able to read
her letter.

'Dear Lily, I spose Len told you I was
cort on the milk-cart. Pore old Badsocks
was cort as well, still snoaring. Mama
and Papa dont no about you. They just
think I ran off. I am being sent to stay
with my cusins to lern speling, sums,
and ladylike behaveyer. Be shore and
right before I go. Love, Lorna.'

Bea bought shoes for Charlie off the rag-and-bone man. Next Tuesday when he delivered the fish up Albert Road he took a letter from Lily, but Lorna wasn't there.

Weeks went by and the letter went backwards and forwards. It got very ragged and at last Charlie lost it.

One day the Lobster didn't come with her order.

'The people at the big house are moving away,' Mr Smith told Pa.

Not long after the house was pulled down. A new road was made, called Albert Crescent, and a lot of new small houses were built.

Trams began running along Albert Road. And motor cars. More and more customers shopped in the High Street. Mr Smith and Pa did a roaring trade.

Bea and Len got married, and Lily was bridesmaid. Pa bought Charlie a *brand new* pair of boots, and they all had their photo taken outside the shop with old Billy.

Lily never quite forgot Lorna. Eating her rabbit pie in the big house, their picnic with Charlie, and rescuing the fish from the flood.

By the time she'd grown up it was just a memory . . . until Lily and Lorna met again. But that is another story.